★ CONTENTS ★

Little Lenny and Witchy-Witch

Well now, there was once a boy called Little Lenny who would never do as he was told.

"You go straight to school," said his mother, "or one of these days Witchy-Witch will get you."

But Little Lenny didn't care about school, or witches either. He dragged his feet and climbed trees.

So, sure enough, one day when he was already late for school, along the road came Witchy-Witch. She saw Little Lenny sitting in a tree and she said to herself, "I'll have that boy."

She put on a voice of sugar and
syrup and called up to him,

*"Dear little boy, sweet little boy,
come down and see what's in
my sack."*

Little Lenny climbed down. And
what do you think was in her
sack? He was!

Quicker than it takes to tell,
Witchy-Witch picked up the sack,
slung it over her shoulder and set
off home.

On the way she passed a field
of potatoes. She was a greedy one,
this one. She said to herself, "A
few potatoes would go well with
boiled boy."

So she put down the sack
and slipped into the field to dig
some up.

Little Lenny took his chance. He wriggled and jiggled his way out of the sack. Then he found a large stone and put it in his place. He tied up the sack, and ran off home, lickety-split.

Soon Witchy-Witch came back, picked up the sack and carried on home.

When she got there she called to her daughter, "Weeny-Witch, put on the pot. We'll have boiled boy for supper."

As soon as the water was ready Witchy-Witch emptied the sack into it.

Splish! Splash! What a crash! The boiling water flew everywhere, all over Witchy-Witch and Weeny-Witch, burning their legs.

"Oh, Mother," squealed Weeny-Witch, "what kind of supper is this? Stone soup! I thought we were having boiled boy."

"And so we shall," said Witchy-Witch, grinding her hard little teeth. "Next time I will have him."

Well now, some people never learn and Little Lenny was one of them.

The very next week there he was again, late for school and hiding up a tree. Along came Witchy-Witch with her sack.

She was in disguise this time and she put on a voice of heather and honey. She called up to Little Lenny,

> *"Dear little boy, sweet little boy,*
> *come down and see what's in*
> *my sack."*

So Little Lenny climbed down
and once again found himself in
the sack.

This time Witchy-Witch tied it
so tight Little Lenny would never
get out.

On the way home she passed a field of parsnips. She said to herself, "A few parsnips would go well with boiled boy."

So she put down the sack and slipped into the field to pull some up.

Little Lenny wriggled and jiggled, but he was caught this time. He started to shout, "Help! Help! Let me out!"

Lucky for him, and he was a
lucky boy, along came a man
with his dog. The man opened the
sack and let him out.

Then Little Lenny told the man
all about the witch and begged
him to put his dog in the sack
instead. The dog wasn't too
pleased, I can tell you.

Well, when Witchy-Witch came
back she picked up the sack and
set off. The sack wriggled and
jiggled on her back. She could
hear a sort of growling.

"No use growling at me, Little
Lenny," she said. "I've caught you
this time."

When she got home Witchy-Witch called her daughter, "Weeny-Witch, have you got the water ready?"

"Yes, Mother," said Weeny-Witch. Her mouth was watering. It was a long time since they'd had boiled boy for supper.

But when they opened the sack, out jumped the dog, who by now was very angry. He bit their ankles; he bit their knees. Then he ran off home to his master.

Witchy-Witch and Weeny-
Witch went without their supper
again.

"Don't worry," Witchy-Witch
told her daughter. "I'll have him
next time."

Can you ever believe it? That Little Lenny still hadn't learned his lesson. The next week he was there again, large as life and looking for trouble.

And he found it.

Down the road came Witchy-Witch in another disguise. When she saw Little Lenny it was "Dear little this" and "Sweet little that" and in no time Little Lenny was back in the sack.

No potatoes or parsnips today. Before you could say 'dithera-dathera-dumplings-and-mash' Witchy-Witch was home.

"We'll take no chances this time," she told her daughter. "Don't take your eyes off him. Put him straight in the oven and bake him."

Then she went out to invite some friends to supper.

"Oh, bother, bother," grumbled Weeny-Witch, who was as lazy as she was stupid. "Come on, let's have you in the oven."

But Little Lenny wasn't stupid. "I'll not fit in there," says he.

"Oh, but you will," says Weeny-Witch.

"Oh, but I won't," says Little Lenny.

"I'll show you," says Weeny-Witch, and she puts her own head inside the oven to show him.

Quick as a thought, Little Lenny comes up behind her and pushes her in. He slams the door and that's the end of her!

But Witchy-Witch is still alive
and here she is, coming back! Just
in time Little Lenny climbs up the
chimney and hides.

When Witchy-Witch comes in she can see neither hide nor hair of her daughter. But by now she's starving hungry, so she says to herself,

"Roasted, toasted, baked or boiled
Better eat him now, before he's
    spoiled."

"You'll have to catch me first,"
shouts Little Lenny.

When Witchy-Witch hears this,
she's furious. She starts to climb up
the chimney after him.

But Little Lenny grabs a loose
brick and throws it at her. Wham!

Then down she falls and lands on her head. That Old Witchy-Witch is STONE DEAD.

But Little Lenny isn't. Lucky
boy!

He's off home, lickety-split.
And that's it.

★ My Own Wee Self ★

There was once a wee lassie
who lived with her mammy in
a wee house all on its lonesome,
ownsome. There was nothing
but the glen below and the
hills beyond.

No one else lived near by, except the wee folk. You know, the fairies and the bogles and the boggarts.

In the evenings the wee lassie
and her mammy ate their supper
of bannocks and cheese.

Then the woman liked to be in
bed before the fire burned low,
before the wee folk were out and
about. You never knew what
harm they might do you.

But would that little lassie of hers go to bed? No, she would not. Ooh, she was a naughty one and always had been.

"Away, lassie, to your bed," said her mammy.

"I will not," said the lassie.

"Aye, you will," said her mammy, "or the wee folk will come and fetch you away."

But the naughty wee lassie
would only laugh and say, "I wish
they would. I'd like one to play
with."

"Whisht," said her mammy,
almost in tears. "What if they
should hear you?"

The wee lassie wasn't in the least put out by her mammy's crying. That's the sort of lassie she was. So she often stayed up warming herself in front of the fire after her mammy had gone up to bed.

Well, now, there came a night,
in the dead of winter, when the
wind tugged at the door and
rattled the windows. The woman
had taken herself to bed as usual.
The wee lassie was sitting there,
all on her lonesome, ownsome.

Suddenly she heard a bit of a sort of rustling in the chimney and down dropped this weeny-wee fairy. She had silvery hair and eyes like green glass and rosy pink cheeks. She was a little beauty.

The naughty wee lassie looked
at the fairy and her mouth
dropped open. When she spoke,
her voice came out in a squeak.
"Oh," she says, "and what would
they be calling you?"

"My own wee self," says the fairy. The fairy's voice was even more of a squeak, but soft and singing too. "And what would they be calling you?" she asks the wee lassie.

"My own wee self too," says the lassie.

Then the two of them started to play together, just as if they were the best of friends and always had been.

The fairy knew some wonderful games. She could make animals out of the ashes and these animals came to life and moved.

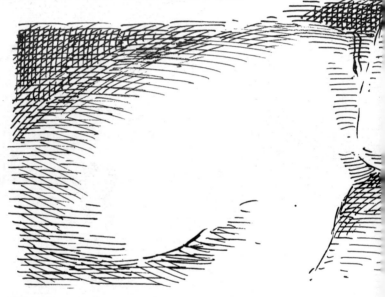

And trees with leaves. And houses, with teeny-weeny wee folk in them, no bigger than your thumbnail. And they could walk and talk, like real folk.

The wee lassie had never seen
anything like it. It was beyond
believing. Now she was glad she
hadn't listened to her mammy.

Soon the fire began to burn
low and she could hardly see the
weeny-wee fairy. She reached for
the poker to stir up the fire.

Suddenly out jumped a red-hot piece of coal. And where do you think it fell? Why, on the weeny-wee foot of the weeny-wee fairy.

Oh, but didn't she squeal!

She squealed so loud it was
like all the wind in all the world
whistling through one teeny-weeny
keyhole.

The wee lassie was so scared she
dropped the poker.

She clapped her hands to her
ears, but that didn't stop the noise.
It got into the wee lassie's head
and swarmed around inside it like
a whole hive of bees.

But then there was another
sound, coming from the chimney.
This time the wee lassie didn't
wait to see what it was. She ran
and hid herself behind her
mammy's chair.

A big booming voice said,
"Who's making that noise?"

"My own wee self," sobbed the
weeny-wee fairy.

"What's wrong with you?" said
the voice.

"Oh, oh, oh, oh," sobbed the
fairy. "It's my weeny-wee foot.
A hot coal burned it."

"And who did it?" asked the voice angrily.

"My own wee self, too, did it," sobbed the weeny-wee fairy, much quieter now.

"Then if you did it your own wee self," cried the voice in the chimney, "what are you making all this fuss about?"

The wee lassie peeped round the arm of the chair just in time to see a big, big hand reach out of the chimney. It caught the weeny-wee fairy by her ear.

It gave her a rough shake and pulled her out of sight up the chimney. The wee lassie heard the fairy's squeals as she disappeared.

Straight away she flew to her
bed, wriggled down under the
covers and made a wee tent for
her own wee self to hide in. For a
long time the wee lassie lay
awake listening, just in case the
fairy-mother should come back.

Now, you'll not be surprised to hear that the next night the wee lassie's mammy had no trouble at all getting her to bed. She went off like a wee lamb. And every night after that the same.

For who could know when a fairy might come to play again and the wee lassie might not get off so easily next time.

It's time for bed
Now put your light out.
I won't tell you twice,
I'm coming... Look out!

There are stories from all over the world about the kinds of things that happen to boys and girls who don't do as they are told. *Little Lenny and Witchy-Witch* is loosely based on an Italian folk tale, while *My Own Wee Self* comes from Scotland.

Here are some more stories you might like to read:

About Witches:

Baba Yaga Bony-Legs
from *The Orchard Book of Magical Tales*
by Margaret Mayo
(Orchard Books)

Hansel and Gretel
from *Grimm's Fairy Tales*

About Sacks:

The Cock, The Mouse and the Little Red Hen
from *The Orchard Book of Nursery Stories*
by Sophie Windham
(Orchard Books)

The Singing Sack
by Helen East
(A&C Black)